I'm Getting
My Act
Together And
Taking It On
The Road

I'm Getting
My Act
Together And
Taking It On
The Road

A Musical

Book & Lyrics by Gretchen Cryer

Music by Nancy Ford

Nelson Doubleday, Inc.
Garden City, New York

I'm Getting My Act Together and Taking It On the Road was first presented by Joseph Papp at the Anspacher Theater of the New York Shakespeare Festival Public Theatre on May 16, 1978. It was directed by Word Baker. The cast, in order of appearance, was as follows:

Joe	Joel Fabiani
Heather	Gretchen Cryer
Alice	Margot Rose
Cheryl	Betty Aberlin
Jake (Acoustic Guitarist)	Don Scardino
Pianist	Scott Berry
Electric Guitarist	Lee Grayson
Percussionist (Drummer)	Bob George
Bassist	Dean Swenson

Orchestrations by Scott Berry, Bob George, Lee Grayson, Don Scardino and Dean Swenson with Nancy Ford.

Orchestration for "Strong Woman Number" by Elliot Weiss.

Orchestrations transcribed by Dean Swenson; copied by Music Preparation International.

MUSICAL NUMBERS

"Natural High"	Heather, Alice, Cheryl and The Liberated Man's Band
"Smile"	Heather, Jake, Cheryl, Alice, and the band
"In A Simple Way I Love You"	Heather and the band
"Miss America"	Heather, Alice, Cheryl
"Strong Woman Number"	Alice, Heather, Cheryl
"Dear Tom"	Heather
"Old Friend"	Heather
Reprise: "In A Simple Way I Love You"	Jake
"Put In A Package And Sold"	Heather, Alice, Cheryl
"If Only Things Was Different"	Jake
"Feel The Love"	The Company
"Lonely Lady"	Heather
"Happy Birthday"	Heather and the band
Reprise: "Natural High"	The Company

NOTES ON THE PRODUCTION

The whole show takes place on the stage of a cabaret music house. It is about a woman "getting her act together"; the act is her life and contains pieces of her past and fragments of her present struggles and viewpoints.

The band consists of five players and two back-up singers. The band members all sing and play various instruments. They also act out the parts of characters in the woman's past; their acting is done at a high-energy slapstick level. Throughout the show there is a constant bantering camaraderie in the band; the musicians are a high-spirited group who provide a constant musical comment and punctuation to the action.

The show is performed on an empty stage—only the instruments and stools are set pieces. Visual changes are accomplished with lights and props. The stools are used throughout to stand on as well as to sit on. Cabaret tables and chairs are on the stage floor.

The performance begins 3–4 minutes before actual curtain time. The house lights stay up through this. The band comes in to warm-up and finish tuning. ALICE and CHERYL are doing stretches. Everyone is chatting quietly and jamming. As soon as JAKE is in place, the group launches into the rehearsal of a song. ALICE, CHERYL, and JAKE are marking the choreography.

I'm Getting
My Act
Together And
Taking It On
The Road

BAND.
GOTTA FEEL THE LOVE
YOU GOTTA GET TO IT
GOTTA FEEL THE PAIN
IF YOU'RE GONNA GET THROUGH IT
YOU CAN'T RUN AWAY
YOU WON'T FIND A PLACE TO HIDE
LET IT BE, LET IT GO
LET IT BE, LET IT GO
LET IT RIDE

GOTTA WALK THE ROAD
YES, YOU GOTTA DO IT
GETTIN' HERE TO THERE
YOU GOTTA GO THROUGH IT
YOU CAN'T RUN AWAY
YOU WON'T FIND A PLACE TO HIDE
LET IT BE, LET IT GO
LET IT BE, LET IT GO
LET IT RIDE—
FEEL THE THING INSIDE

(*Instrumental—then they repeat the last verse. The* TECH-
NICIANS, *a* STAGE MANAGER, *a* FOLLOW SPOT OPERATOR,

a Sound Person *and an* Electrician *are at their posts.*
As the Band *is finishing this song,* Heather's Manager,
a good-looking guy in his thirties enters hurriedly.)

Manager. Okay, let's get started, 'cause I haven't heard a
lot of this stuff.

Jake. Hi Joe.

Manager. Oh hi Jake, where's Heather?

Jake. Gee, I don't know . . .

Heather. (*Hurrying in. She hugs him joyously.*) Joe,
you're back, I've missed you. How was L.A.?

Manager. Great, great. Got in this morning. (*Through
this there is kissing and holding.* Heather *gets on to the
stage platform.*)

Heather. How's your group doing out there?

Manager. Oooh . . . terrible.

Heather. Oooh . . .

Band. Oooh . . .

Manager. Well, we've still got half the album to cut, but
I wanted to get back for your opening.

Heather. You better.

MANAGER. Hey, listen, if things go well here I think I can get you into the Troubador out there. (ALL *ad lib greats, oohs, etc., not a big reaction, short and sweet.*)

HEATHER. (*Calling up to the light booth.*) Hey Isabella!

ISABELLA. (*The Stage Manager.*) Yeah Heather.

HEATHER. Kill the house lights.

ISABELLA. You got it. (*The house lights go out.*)

MANAGER. (*To* HEATHER.) Hey, you look different. What did you do to your hair?

HEATHER. I just let it go. This is the way it is.

MANAGER. Hey, I like it. It looks great. But your fans out there in TV land are used to seeing you with it straight.

HEATHER. Yeah, see, that's what I wanted to talk to you about . . .

MANAGER. We'll talk about it later, it's easy to fix. Okay, what have you got for me.

HEATHER. A lot of new stuff.

MANAGER. Great. Got enough for a new album?

HEATHER. Yeah. I don't know if it's album material, though.

MANAGER. Listen, who knows? Anything goes these days.

The band knows that. (*Looking at* LEE.) Right, Len? Lou? Lee! Those bastards at RCA are gonna wish they never let you go. I been talking to Atlantic. Am I gonna like this stuff? Sure I'm gonna like it.

HEATHER. I don't know. I'm a little nervous.

MANAGER. Well I trust you. You have impeccable taste. Okay, let's see it. Tonight's the big night.

HEATHER. (*Calling up to the follow spot.*) Josephine, are you there?

JOSEPHINE. There you go Heather. (*The spot hits* HEATHER.)

HEATHER. (*Calling up to the* SOUND OPERATOR.) Greg? (*She taps the microphone.*)

GREG. Make it happen, sweetheart.

MANAGER. Listen, that's not what you're going to wear tonight, is it?

HEATHER. (*Laughing.*) I don't know. Maybe.

MANAGER. Well, all I can say is eeek. (*They laugh.*)

HEATHER. We'll start this in the dark and Jake will make the announcement over the intro . . .

JAKE. (*Into the microphone.*) Heather Jones and the Liberated Men's Band

CHERYL and ALICE. Plus Two

HEATHER. And then we just start.

MANAGER. Let's do it. (*The* BAND *begins.*) Announcement, announcement, blah, blah, blah, Heather Jones and the Liberated Men's Band Plus Two. (*He looks around and finds the* ASSISTANT STAGE MANAGER. *Calling to her.*) Honey, can you get me a ginger ale? (*She goes off.*)

HEATHER.
THAT PHONE JUST KEEPS ON RINGIN'
THEN SOMEBODY'S AT MY DOOR
I FEEL ALL PULLED TO PIECES
CAN'T FIND INSPIRATION ANY MORE
THERE'S SO MANY PEOPLE LEANING ON ME
I'M GETTING RUN INTO THE GROUND
EVERYBODY'S WANTING SOMETHING FROM ME
AND THERE'S NOT ENOUGH OF ME TO
    GO AROUND
BUT TOMORROW I HIT THE ROAD
GONNA LET LOOSE OF THIS HEAVY LOAD AND

ALL.
FLY

MUSIC IS MY ONE SALVATION
SINGING IS MY CELEBRATION
AND PLAYING WITH A ROCK 'N ROLL BAND
IS A NATURAL HIGH

HEATHER. (*During the musical break in the song.*) Joe, a spot is going to be on me and lots of color on the band.

MANAGER. OK OK I've heard this. (*The* BAND *lowers its volume to hear what* JOE *is saying.*) The tape you sent me when I was out on the coast. (HEATHER *nods her remembrance.* JOE *calls to the* BAND.) Just cut to the last verse. I want to hear how it ends.

HEATHER. We'll skip to the last verse, cut right to the end. (ALL *get ready in new positions for the end and figure out where they are musically.* HEATHER *takes her microphone off the Center stand and moves to sit on Left bench, calling up to the* STAGE MANAGER.) Lights.
ALL I NEED IS A LITTLE ROOM
A PLACE THAT IS FINE AND FREE
A ROOM WHERE I CAN THINK TO MYSELF
WHERE NOBODY'S NEEDING ME
AND THEN I'LL FIND MY WAY AGAIN
AND I WILL SING MY SONG

TRIO.
AND I'LL FIND THE JOY AGAIN
THAT COMES WHEN I'M FEELING STRONG

HEATHER.
SO TOMORROW I HIT THE ROAD
GONNA LET LOOSE OF THIS HEAVY LOAD AND

ALL.
FLY

MUSIC IS MY ONE SALVATION
SINGIN' IS MY CELEBRATION
AND PLAYIN' WITH A ROCK 'N ROLL BAND
IS A NATURAL HIGH
OOO

(*The song fades to nothing as though a little rock 'n roll band is going down the road into the distance. The* DRUMMER *sounds a wind chime at the end of the song.*)

MANAGER. Applause, applause. Honey that's nice. It's nice but I'm not sure about it as an opener. It starts kind of down.

HEATHER. But it gets up—the chorus gets up.

JOE. But then it ends with this little wistful thing at the end.

HEATHER. It's supposed to be wistful—a little rock 'n roll band going down the road—Sort of Fellini. (BOBBY, *the* DRUMMER, *sounds the wind chimes again to demonstrate.* JOE *looks up at him. Chimes stop.*)

MANAGER. Yeah, but that brings everybody down. Since it's your first number, you should leave them up. Try this, do the chorus and end up. (HEATHER, *allowing this, goes up to the* BAND.)

SCOTT. (*The Pianist.*) Where do you want to take it from, Heather?

HEATHER. So tomorrow I hit the road. (*To the* WOMEN.) You take the high vocals. (*To* JAKE.) And you and I will double on the ending.

HEATHER and GROUP.
SO TOMORROW I HIT THE ROAD

GONNA LET LOOSE OF THIS HEAVY LOAD AND
   FLY
MUSIC IS MY ONE SALVATION
SINGIN' IS MY CELEBRATION
AND PLAYIN' WITH A ROCK 'N ROLL BAND
IS A NATURAL HIGH

(*The* BAND *ends with a big flourish, a snap ending. Pause.
Then the* PIANO PLAYER *begins a rinky-tink version of*
"THERE'S NO BUSINESS LIKE SHOW BUSINESS"
and the BAND *joins in.* BOBBY *is blowing soap bubbles.*)

MANAGER. Okay, okay, you guys. Settle down. Bobby,
bubbles. We've got a talented drummer—he doubles on
bubbles. That ending was much better. That's the way we'll
do it. Now, Heather, what are you going to say? Say it the
way you're going to say it tonight.

HEATHER. Hello, I'm Heather Jones. I'm going to be
doing songs tonight that I've written with the group.
They're personal songs. But we wanted to do something
kind of different, so we're including some sketches—the
group is full of terrific actors. When I was growing up in the
fifties—there was an entirely—

MANAGER. Wait a minute. Hold it. Honey, I wouldn't say
that about the fifties.

HEATHER. What's wrong with that?

MANAGER. Just leave it out. I don't think you need it.

HEATHER. But I did grow up in the fifties.

MANAGER. Yeah, but nobody has to know it.

HEATHER. What's wrong with growing up in the fifties?

MANAGER. Well, it just kind of limits your appeal.

HEATHER. Look, today is my birthday. (*The* BAND *plays a cut-time version of "HAPPY BIRTHDAY."* JAKE *hugs* HEATHER.)

MANAGER. Oh yeah? I forgot. Shit.

HEATHER. I'm thirty-nine.

MANAGER. Jesus . . . Well, happy birthday anyway.

HEATHER. Thank you.

MANAGER. Look, honey, nobody has to know that. On the soap opera you don't play thirty-nine . . . Oh you're not thirty-nine. You're putting me on. How long have I known you? Let's see, in '73 you were thirty—

HEATHER. I was lying! I'm thirty-nine! Look at these lines in my face. And this morning I found a gray hair.

MANAGER. Yeah, but under the lights . . . we'll fix it with the lights. Nobody will see those lines. Don't worry.

HEATHER. I'm not worried! Who said I was worried!? *You're* worried! You're the one.

MANAGER. I'm not worried. It's just that I didn't know you were thirty-nine. It just kind of took me off-guard. I mean I know that sometimes you look like you've been through the wringer, but . . .

HEATHER. I look like I've been through the wringer because I *have* been through the wringer! That's who I *am!* A person who's been through the wringer! I can't pretend I haven't been through the wringer!

MANAGER. Calm down, sweetie. Look, I'm not asking you to pretend that you haven't been through the wringer. It's just that . . . well, I don't know how I'm going to sell that. I mean, gray hair and lines in the face.

HEATHER. Paul Newman has lines in his face. Steve McQueen. Charles Bronson. Charles Bronson has definitely been through the wringer.

MANAGER. Yeah, but honey that's different.

HEATHER. Why is it different? Why? Why?

MANAGER. You are not in the same bag as Charles Bronson. Let's face it, honey, Olivia Newton John does not have wrinkles. Linda Ronstadt does not have wrinkles.

HEATHER. Well, it's very obvious what the problem is.

MANAGER. Look, honey, there's no problem. You're just uptight because it's your opening night and you're thirty-nine.

HEATHER. No, there is a very definite problem here. It's a sexual problem.

MANAGER. You have a sexual problem. Look, nobody has to know about that either.

HEATHER. Men can have lines in their faces and gray hair and it's sexy but in women it's not sexy. Why is that?! Why is that?!

MANAGER. Look, sweetheart, I don't know.

HEATHER. Well, I'll tell you why. Men are allowed to have lines in their faces because it makes them look like they have lived and have had experience and that's very attractive in a man. It's sexy. But it's not attractive in a woman.

MANAGER. That's right. But don't worry about it. We can fix it with the lights. Go on to the second number.

HEATHER. Okay, but we'll talk about this later. (*The* BAND *begins a nostalgic waltz, like a music box.*)
DADDY ALWAYS SAID I WASN'T PRETTY
UNLESS I WOULD SMILE

HE SAID, "SMILE"
SO I'D SMILE, SMILE, SMILE

I WAS DADDY'S SMILING GIRL
I ALWAYS TRIED TO PLEASE
I COULD MAKE HIM HAPPY
AND PUT HIM AT HIS EASE
I WOULD SMILE FOR DADDY
AND SING A LITTLE SONG

AND DADDY WOULD TAKE CARE OF ME
THAT'S HOW WE GOT ALONG

HE SAID, "SMILE"
SO I'D SMILE, SMILE, SMILE

(HEATHER'S MOTHER *appears played by* CHERYL. *She wears a party hat and is dressed in a forties dress. The scenes are done in a high-energy slapstick fashion. Throughout the dialogue* ALICE *supplies all the props for the action.*)

MOTHER. Happy birthday, honey. How does it feel to be five years old? Where's your party hat? Oh, here it is. Put it on.

HEATHER. (*Pushing away her party hat.*) I don't want to have a party. The kids act so silly.

MOTHER. But they're your friends. And you *must* act nice to your friends. Last week when Uncle Herman was here, you were not nice to him. He was very hurt.

HEATHER. He kept pinching me on the bottom.

MOTHER. But that is no reason for you to bite him. I will not have it.

(HEATHER'S FATHER, *played by* JAKE, *joins* HEATHER *and* CHERYL *and tries to pinch* MOTHER'S *bottom. She is*

*unresponsive. He is in a very gay mood and talks baby
talk to his wife.*)

FATHER. How's the little mother? . . . Mmm . . . isn't
she purty? She's the best looking little mother.

MOTHER. (*Pulling away.*) Oh John, don't act so silly.

FATHER. (*Still the baby talk.*) And there's my little birthday girl. She sure looks purty too.

HEATHER. Mommy, why aren't you nice to Daddy? You
don't let him hug you. You never do. Why is that?

MOTHER. I'm tired. Tired to the bone.

FATHER. (*Smiling jovially.*) Mother's just irked. She's always irked with Daddy. But she sure is purty. And Daddy
sure does love her. Someday Daddy's going to buy her
beautiful clothes and get her a beautiful car and make her
happy. Right, Mother?

MOTHER. That'll be the day. (ALICE *hands* JAKE *a
1940's camera.*)

FATHER. Okay, how's about a picture. Daddy John wants
to take a picture of his little girl on her fifth birthday. Smile
for Daddy. (HEATHER *manages a smile for her* DADDY *and*
DADDY *snaps a picture.*) Smile! That's a good girl.

BAND.
SMILE, SMILE, SMILE
SMILE, SMILE
    (JAKE *returns the camera to* ALICE.)

HEATHER.
I WAS DADDY'S FAVORITE GIRL
I ALWAYS TRIED TO PLEASE
I COULD MAKE HIM HAPPY
AND PUT HIM AT HIS EASE
HE SAID "SMILE"
SO I'D SMILE, SMILE, SMILE

(*During the last smile sequence* ALICE *has put a mortar board on* HEATHER'S *head.*)

MOTHER. Dad and I sure are proud of you honey.

FATHER. (*Still talking a kind of fond baby talk.*) Well, here's my high school graduate. Yep, Daddy sure does have a leader on his hands. Straight A's, editor of the newspaper, best singer in the choir. She's a geeenius. Put your tassel on the right side genie, weenie. (*He changes the tassel from left to right.*)

HEATHER. Daddy, why do you always talk baby talk to me? Just say it. Just say what you have to say.

FATHER. Aw, honey, get off my back. You're getting to be like your mother. C'mon, everybody gang up on Daddy.

MOTHER. Oh, John.

HEATHER. We're not ganging up.

FATHER. What's a matter? Can't I be proud of my little daughter? Let your poor ole pappy have some glory. Look at that report card. Got brains like a man. My daughter is a leader. That's what it said in the newspaper. Leader. Leader.

HEATHER. Right, Daddy, I'm a leader.

FATHER. Everybody jump on Daddy. Jeez . . . ! I don't know what it is. When I'm around everybody gets itchy. What is it? I come into the kitchen and I hear Mother singing but as soon as she knows I'm in the room she stops. Silence. The cold shoulder. Everybody's got it in for Daddy.

MOTHER. (*Tired.*) Nobody's got it in for you, John.

FATHER. I guess it must be female hormones or something. I never have understood women. What does it take to make you happy?

MOTHER. I don't know, John.

HEATHER. Daddy, if you're going to take this picture, go ahead and take it, 'cause I've got to go. I've got a date.

FATHER. Okay, little daughter. Why don't you hold the electric mixer you won for being the best public speaker in the state. Here it is. Just hold it in one hand with your diploma in the other.

HEATHER. Daddy, this is going to look stupid.

FATHER. C'mon. I want a picture of my genius holding her electric mixer.

HEATHER. Okay, just take the picture.

FATHER. (*Still focusing his camera.*) Who's the lucky guy that gets to go out with the genius tonight?

HEATHER. Tommy.

FATHER. I wonder how he feels going out with a genius. Don't act too smart, you know. Or you'll never get to use your mixer on him.

HEATHER. Sure, Daddy.

FATHER. Okay, smile. (*He takes the picture. Flash. The* BAND *bursts in singing.*)

BAND.
SMILE, SMILE, SMILE
SMILE, SMILE

TRIO.
IF YOU SMILE IN JUST THE RIGHT WAY
YOU'LL MAKE A PRETTY WIFE
AND SOMEONE WILL TAKE CARE OF YOU
FOR ALL YOUR PRETTY LIFE
IF YOU SMILE, SMILE, SMILE
IF YOU SMILE

(*Lights change on* HEATHER. *She is in a wedding veil. It's her wedding day. She is with her* MOTHER *who is working on the hem of the veil.*)

HEATHER. Mom, have you been happy with Dad?

MOTHER. As happy as could be expected I guess. But then I don't think you can necessarily expect to be happy.

HEATHER. Tommy and I are going to be happy. I know it.

MOTHER. Well . . . life is a compromise. The woman has to go 75 percent of the way because the man will only go 25 percent, if that much.

HEATHER. Mother, that's awful.

MOTHER. That's the way it is, honey. You can't change it.

HEATHER. I don't believe that.

MOTHER. You just have to muddle through. Look at your father. He does exactly what he wants, come hell or high water. I didn't want that new pick-up. I didn't want the buzz saw. I didn't want him to drill for oil in my rose garden. I didn't want any of it. People pounding on the door day and night. Using my bathroom.

HEATHER. So if you're not happy with Daddy, why don't you leave, Mother? Just leave.

MOTHER. Where would I go? Life is not a bowl of cherries. Never has been. Never will be.

HEATHER. You should tell Daddy how you feel.

MOTHER. Wouldn't do any good. He tunes me out. He just hears what he wants to hear . . . But there's the good side. At least he doesn't drink like my father did. That's a blessing. I prayed and prayed that my father would die before mother so that she could have a little time to herself, a little time to be happy. But he didn't, he held on, the old coot. Finally she died first and he died the next day. He just couldn't let her have anything. Well, anyway, honey, Dad and I sure want you to be happy. Maybe the next generation can do better. It's too late for me.

(LEE, *the* LEAD GUITAR PLAYER, *comes down to join* HEATHER *Center Stage. He carries the acoustic guitar and has a bow tie collar on. He is the* BRIDEGROOM. SCOTT *has gotten into a full-length minister's robe and stands on the piano.*)

MINISTER. (SCOTT.) June 15, 1958. Do you take this man to be your lawfully wedded husband for better or worse, in sickness and health, to love and obey, to be his help-mate, build him up when he's down, bear his children, send his pants to the cleaners, pick his underwear up off the floor, hold a job that'll bring in a little extra money but which won't absorb you to the point where you won't be able to have supper ready at six o'clock every night, and cleave to him only 'til death do you part? (*Drum roll.*)

HEATHER. I do. (*Cymbal crash.*)

MINISTER. I now pronounce you man and wife. Let's see a big smile for your husband.

ALL. Smile, smile, smile.

HEATHER. I'm going to make you happy, Tommy. *We're going to be happy!*

(*The* BAND *plays a fanfare and the traditional wedding*

recessional. ALICE *throws confetti from her bowler into the air over* HEATHER. HEATHER *smiles and tosses the bouquet over head to* ALICE.)

BAND. (*Over the recessional.*)
SMILE, SMILE, SMILE

(DADDY *puts his arm around* TOMMY *and pulls him aside conspiratorially.*)

FATHER. All right, Tom, my son, I want you to take good care of my little girl. She's the apple of her daddy's eye. I'm giving her over to you now, boy, and I want you to support her in the manner to which she has been accustomed. And if you need any hints about tonight I'll be glad to help you out.

TOMMY. Thank you, sir, but I think I can handle it.

FATHER. And if you need any cash— (*Feeling for his wallet.*) Oh, I guess Mother has my wallet—

TOMMY. No, that's all right, sir.

FATHER. Well, good luck. Be good to her, son. Keep her smiling.

BAND.
SMILE, SMILE, SMILE
SMILE, SMILE

HEATHER.
NOW I WAS TOMMY'S SMILING GIRL
I ALWAYS TRIED TO PLEASE
I COULD MAKE HIM HAPPY
AND PUT HIM AT HIS EASE
I WOULD SMILE FOR TOMMY
AND SING A LITTLE SONG
AND TOMMY WOULD TAKE CARE OF ME
THAT'S HOW WE GOT ALONG

HE SAID, "SMILE"
SO I'D SMILE, SMILE, SMILE

BAND.
HE SAID, "SMILE"
SO I'D SMILE, SMILE, SMILE SMILE SMILE

(*The music goes into a whole cake-walk thing, a black-face minstrel dance with* CHERYL, HEATHER, *and* JAKE. ALL THREE *wear straw hats and gloves.* ALICE *puts a glitter band on her bowler.* JAKE *plays the banjo,* ALICE *is playing the tambourine. The* WOMEN *are smiling to please in old-style "darkie" fashion. When the dance is finished they all bow. As the lights come up the* MANAGER *is walking up to* HEATHER *shaking his head in disbelief. Long pause.*)

HEATHER. You didn't like it.

MANAGER. I liked it. Oh, I liked it. But . . . Look, honey, I got people coming from the trades tonight—big people—

critics, the radio stations. I don't know what you're trying to do here.

HEATHER. I told you I wanted to try something different and you said go ahead, that we had nothing to lose at this point. That's what you said.

MANAGER. I know that's what I said, but—

HEATHER. It's an explanation of where I'm coming from.

MANAGER. Right . . .

HEATHER. I'm trying to define myself for the audience.

MANAGER. Yeah, well, it's okay to be different, but all these scenes— Nobody does scenes in their nightclub act. We might as well go home and watch TV, you know what I mean.

HEATHER. Look, a lot of people do strange things. Alice Cooper. Alice used to have snakes in his act. Now that was unusual.

MANAGER. Look honey, snakes are one thing, that's something people can identify with. It's freaky and there are a lot of freaks out there. But your thing is not freaky, it's just offensive.

HEATHER. Who does it offend?

MANAGER. It offends me and it's gonna offend your audience. That minstrel show thing is definitely going to offend your blacks.

HEATHER. But didn't you get the point? Maybe it's not clear. I could fix that.

MANAGER. It's clear that it's offensive. And all that stuff in the marriage ceremony about picking up his underwear—

that's going to offend your men. I mean, men don't like to be reminded about their underwear, you know what I mean? There's a lot in there that's going to offend your men in the audience.

HEATHER. That was just one little line in there. Why did you pick that one out? Do you not pick up your underwear?

MANAGER. I pick up my underwear! And that's not all. I support my wife. And I have to remind her to get the groceries. And I got a cleaning lady. She never cooks. What does she want? Look, I don't want to be psychoanalyzed here. It's no big deal. Everything's fine. My relationship with Francesca is better than it's ever been. It's just that there are getting to be a lot of offensive women around these days—ball-breakers . . . you know what I mean? Now I know you're not, honey, but I just don't want you in that bag. Olivia Newton-John is not a ball-breaker. Linda Ronstadt is not a ball-breaker.

HEATHER. Why don't you ask Francesca what she wants?

MANAGER. She doesn't know. She's confused. She wants to be taken care of, but she wants her freedom. I'm a sucker, right?

HEATHER. I don't know her that well.

MANAGER. Believe me, I'm a sucker. But I'm not alone.

There are a lot of us suckers out there. My looks are deceiving, you know. I mean, I look like a tough macho guy, you know what I mean—but inside I'm a cream-puff. I wish I could be hard, tough. Charles Bronson is not a sucker.

HEATHER. Well, I don't know Charles Bronson . . .

MANAGER. Look, honey, I'm not feeling too good today. Maybe it's jet lag. Look do me a favor, will you? Do that number from the old act that I love so much. It would be good right in this spot. It's always been a grabber.

HEATHER. Are you talking about "In A Simply Way I Love You"?

MANAGER. Yeah, that's the one. Do it. It'll calm my nerves.

HEATHER. I'm really tired of that song, Joe.

MANAGER. Honey, I know what I'm talking about. Middle America will love it.

HEATHER. Joe, I don't even like that song anymore, and it definitely does not go in my new act.

MANAGER. But you owe it to your fans to do something of yours that's familiar to them. DO IT! (*The* BAND *is confused.*)

HEATHER. Okay.

SCOTT. Which key, Heather?

HEATHER. D, I guess . . .
IN A SIMPLE WAY I LOVE YOU

MANAGER. That's it.

HEATHER.
I'M HERE TO SEE YOU THROUGH

MANAGER. It's beautiful. (*And he starts to hum along.*)

HEATHER.
I WILL LISTEN WHILE YOU SING YOUR SONG
WHILE YOU DO WHAT YOU HAVE TO DO

MANAGER. It's great, baby. It's the only thing you had
that ever hit the charts.

HEATHER.
IN A SIMPLE WAY I LOVE YOU—
It was number 89
YOU'RE ALL MY LIFE TO ME
I WILL BE THERE WHEN YOU NEED A FRIEND

MANAGER. This is what they want to hear. It's beautiful.

HEATHER.
I'LL HELP YOU BE WHAT YOU WANT TO BE
I'LL STAND BEHIND YOU
RAIN OR SHINE
YOU ARE MY EVERYTHING
I'M YOURS AND YOU ARE MINE
Joe, I can't keep doing this.

(*The music continues full force with the back-up* VOICES *ooohing passionately on.*)

MANAGER. C'mon baby, it sounds great. What's the matter?

HEATHER. I may throw up.

MANAGER. It's beautiful— (*He sings to try to encourage her.*)
MY EVERY DREAM COME TRUE

HEATHER. My every dream, my every dream!— What does that mean? That means nothing. It's oatmeal. (HEATHER *turns and cuts off the* BAND. *They dribble to a halt.*)

MANAGER. Well, you wrote it. What's the matter, has some guy been giving you a hard time again?

HEATHER. That is irrelevant!

MANAGER. Babe, I feel for you, but you can't let your personal feelings get in the way of the material. I mean we all have our ups and downs.

HEATHER. It's just that this song doesn't mean anything to me any more. I wrote it a long time ago, in another life. It's Jello.

MANAGER. Look, it may be Jello, but Jello's pretty. We need some beauty in our lives, babe, some fantasy. Something to brighten our dreary days and nights. Everybody needs that. Cheryl, could you get me an Alka-Seltzer?

HEATHER. I puke on it!

MANAGER. Do you want an Alka-Seltzer?

HEATHER. No!

MANAGER. Look, do you want to talk about your problems? I mean something is obviously hanging you up here.

HEATHER. No, I can handle it.

MANAGER. Sometimes it helps to talk. We've talked in the past when you were falling apart—

HEATHER. Who's falling apart?

MANAGER. Okay, okay. I was just offering a comforting shoulder, a little warmth.

HEATHER. Well, thank you. Look, you've always been terrific and I appreciate that, Joe. But right now I just want to show you the rest of my new stuff.

MANAGER. Okay, okay. I just want you to know I'm here for you if you need me.

HEATHER. Right.

MANAGER. All right, let's see what you've got and then we'll see if we can save it.

HEATHER. And listen, Joe, I'm sorry I wasn't too sympathetic about your problems with Francesca. But she seems like such a child and I just can't relate to that. Actually I hate it. And you cater to it. But still, I'm sorry you're feeling bad.

MANAGER. Don't worry. I can handle it. It's my problem. Just go ahead. What are you gonna say before your next number?

HEATHER. Josephine. Let's use the spot on this . . . (*A spot picks her up.*) Well, I'm going to say, "I'm standing here at the beginning of my fortieth year . . ."

MANAGER. Christ! Say thirty-nine, it doesn't sound as bad as forty.

HEATHER. I'm standing here on my thirty-ninth birthday wondering if it is at all possible for men and women to have decent constructive relationships with each other when our culture and our past so conspire against it—when we can hardly pick our way through the myths and distortions of what we are. Our very definitions of love depend upon the extent to which we "feel like a man" or "feel like a woman" and the extent to which we feel like a man or woman depends upon our culture's definition of what it is to be a man or woman. And so what feels like love is often a function of how well we are fulfilling our culture's stereotypes of what it is to be a man or woman. And if we start breaking the stereotypes and redefining ourselves, then the way we relate to others is not going to feel like love—or like what love has been defined as in the past . . . See.

MANAGER. Christ!

ALL.
MISS AMERICA

HEATHER.
MISS AMERICA
WHERE ARE YOU TODAY?
FOUR KIDS AND A HUSBAND
YOUR TROPHIES TUCKED AWAY
SITTING IN YOUR DREAM HOUSE
WATCHING THE TV
THINKING HOW THINGS NEVER ARE
THE WAY YOU THOUGHT THEY'D BE

TRIO.
MISS AMERICA
LONG AGO AND FAR AWAY
MISS AMERICA
WHERE ARE YOU TODAY?

HEATHER.
THEY TOLD YOU YOU HAD EVERYTHING
THEY SAID YOU WERE A QUEEN
AND EVERYBODY ENVIED YOU
WHEN YOU WERE JUST EIGHTEEN
BUT NOW YOU'RE FEELING DESPERATE
CAUSE YOU CAN'T STAY EVER YOUNG
THEY NEVER TOLD YOU WHAT TO DO
WHEN YOU PASSED THIRTY ONE

LADIES TRIO.
MISS AMERICA
LONG AGO AND FAR AWAY
MISS AMERICA
WHERE ARE YOU TODAY?

BEAUTY WAS YOUR CURRENCY
TALENT WAS YOUR STYLE

LOVERS FALLING AT YOUR FEET
POWER IN YOUR SMILE

YOU MARRIED SOMEONE JUST LIKE YOU
HE WAS A GOLDEN CATCH
AND EVERYBODY ENVIED YOU
IT WAS A PERFECT MATCH

HEATHER.
NOW YOU'RE SITTIN' IN YOUR DREAM HOUSE
WATCHING THE TV
THINKING HOW THINGS NEVER ARE
THE WAY YOU THOUGHT THEY'D BE
YOUR HUSBAND'S OFF ON BUSINESS
HIS BUSINESS IS HIS LIFE
HE PRETENDS TO BE YOUR HUSBAND
YOU PRETEND TO BE HIS WIFE

TRIO.
MISS AMERICA
HOW DID IT SLIP AWAY
MISS AMERICA
WHERE ARE YOU TODAY?

HEATHER.
CAUSE IT'S NOT FOREVER AFTER
AND YOU'VE FINALLY LOST YOUR HOPE
AND YOU'RE FEELING LIKE AN ACTRESS
IN YOUR OWN DEPRESSING SOAP
AND YOU THINK YOU'RE GOING CRAZY
AND YOU'RE SCARED OF GETTING FREE
AND YOU'D LIKE TO TAKE YOUR TROPHY
AND SMASH THE DAMN TV!

TRIO.
MISS AMERICA
NO WONDER YOU FEEL BAD
YOU BOUGHT THE STUFF THEY SOLD YOU
AND BABY, YOU'VE BEEN HAD

HEATHER.
YOU RULED THE LAND OF NEVER-WAS
A PRINCESS IN A PLAY
BUT YOU'VE GOT TIME, IT'S NOT TOO LATE
YOU'VE STILL GOT TODAY

TRIO and MEN.
MISS AMERICA
YOU'VE GOT THINGS TO DO
MISS AMERICA
IT'S ALL INSIDE OF YOU

MISS AMERICA
YOU CAN FIND A WAY
MISS AMERICA YOU'VE STILL GOT TODAY
MISS AMERICA!

(*The* WOMEN *break and arrange the stools to simulate a table where they are sitting.*)

HEATHER. God damn it! I've spent my whole life improving myself until I am a magnificent person and no one, NO ONE wants to share my life.

ALICE. Something is fucked.

CHERYL. Definitely.

HEATHER. I mean what is it with us—here we are three wonderful, beautiful, talented people . . .

MANAGER. Heather . . .

HEATHER. Joe . . . Here we are three wonderful, beautiful, talented people . . .

ALICE. Independent, running our own lives . . .

MANAGER. Cool it Alice, I have to talk to Heather . . . Honey, the song is great, I love it. But you're insulting the audience that is coming to see you.

HEATHER. I am not.

MANAGER. I mean "Miss America, sitting in your dream house, you're going to take your trophy and smash the damn TV"? Honey, we're sold out all across the country to those people who watch you on the TV. Procter and Gamble is going to shit.

HEATHER. Joe, you just walked into the middle of one of our scenes.

MANAGER. Another scene? Jesus.

HEATHER. The three of us got together and wrote this scene . . .

MANAGER. (*Pointing to* ALICE.) What's she got on?

HEATHER. It's a tool vest. She's playing a character who's building her own . . .

HEATHER, ALICE and CHERYL. Loftbed.

MANAGER. Why? Why? Why?

HEATHER. It's a scene about three strong . . .

ALICE. independent . . .

CHERYL. single women,

HEATHER. talking about their

HEATHER, ALICE and CHERYL. mutual problems.

HEATHER. It's very relevant. So sit down and listen. Okay?

CHERYL. Where from?

HEATHER. (*To the* WOMEN.) From the top. (*They go very quickly through the part they've already done and then continue on at a proper speed.*) God damn it! I've spent my whole life improving myself until I am a magnificent person and no one, no one wants to share my life.

ALICE. Something is fucked.

CHERYL. Definitely.

HEATHER. I mean what is it with us—here we are three wonderful, beautiful, talented people—

ALICE. independent, running our own lives—

HEATHER. —I mean, I have *created* this apartment by my-self. With my own hands I have wrought something out of nothing—

ALICE. I went to the God-damn evening classes, at the New School for God's sake, and learned carpentry—

CHERYL. I took electrical wiring. I can solder.

HEATHER. Well, here we are—

ALICE. —three fantastic human beings—

CHERYL. —and those assholes don't want to be with us.

HEATHER. I don't get it.

CHERYL. (*To* ALICE.) When is Frank coming back into town?

ALICE. Do I know? I never know. He's got a play opening here in a couple of months.

CHERYL. Emilio is out in Colorado I think for a few weeks. He says he needs space.

ALICE. I may not see Frank for three months and then suddenly he calls up in the middle of the night from London and says he's going to be in town. And then I always see him and it's always wonderful. And then he always leaves and goes back to his wife.

HEATHER. Jim told me I was the most wonderful woman he had ever known. He even made up a list—on one side he put what he gets from me and on the other side he put what he gets from his wife. *He couldn't think of anything he gets from his wife!* It's come to that. And yet, where is he? Right back there with his wife.

CHERYL. But Emilio doesn't even have a wife. He leaves anyway. He says he feels threatened if I come in to his space.

ALICE. See, I think somebody's lying. We don't know the whole truth here.

CHERYL. I mean, do I look like someone who would threaten someone's space?

HEATHER. You're right, you're right. They're probably lying. But I didn't *feel* Jim was lying. See, I just can't trust my feelings.

CHERYL. So there he is out in the desert with all this space around him—

HEATHER. No, see, we have to face it. All this doesn't mean shit. It doesn't matter how wonderful we are—

ALICE. It doesn't matter if I can build my own loftbed. It doesn't matter if I've pulled myself up by my own boot-straps—

HEATHER. —because people just are with who they're with and there's no sense to it.

CHERYL. Or else they're just *not* with who they're with . . .

ALICE. It doesn't have anything to do with how wonderful a person is.

CHERYL. I mean, do I look threatening? If you saw me coming down the street, would you say that's a threatening person?

HEATHER. Jim said he liked the way I smelled. And he said that his wife had started going for days without taking a shower. She'd come home from her exercise class and leave her stinky leotards all over.

ALICE. But see, that doesn't matter. Obviously it doesn't matter.

HEATHER. And she doesn't water the plants when he's gone. His plants were dying when he was away doing his research. And my plants are terrific. He could see my plants are terrific.

ALICE. I know, I know! *My* plants are terrific. It's a jungle in there. I have to go in there with a machete.

HEATHER. And she says Jim doesn't turn her on. So she has another lover. And he and I have a wonderful sexual relationship.

ALICE. Yeah, Frank's and mine is the best.

CHERYL. Emilio says I am the most passionate lover he's ever had.

HEATHER. And she doesn't feed the cats or empty the litter box. He had to *hire* somebody to do it when he was gone.

CHERYL. And yet where is he—all alone with his horse and his gun. I think he has a fear of intimacy.

HEATHER. I think I'd like to have a confrontation with Jim and say, "Why is it, why is it? Tell me. Tell me the truth. You said I was the most wonderful woman in the world, so why don't you want me? Here I am, making my own way, I'm successful in my own profession, I can handle my own life, you like the way I smell, we have terrific times together, but you prefer to be with the one who says someone else turns her on, who doesn't hold a job, who doesn't water the plants, who doesn't change the cat litter and who leaves her stinky leotards all over."

CHERYL. It's a fear of intimacy. (*Long pause.*)

HEATHER. The question becomes . . . Why do I want to be with someone who doesn't want to be with me?

CHERYL. Yeah, why is that?

ALICE. What do we get out of that?

HEATHER. Well, we get to be alone. And we get to be strong. It's a terrific image.

ALICE. Yeah, I kinda like this image—the strong woman building her own life.

MANAGER. Heather, honey, it's a good scene . . .

HEATHER. Thank you.

MANAGER. Very well written . . .

HEATHER. Thank you.

MANAGER. But it's long.

HEATHER. Joe, a song comes right here.

MANAGER. And actually, the image of these three women is not too attractive. I mean you're like a bunch of . . . I don't know what it is you're like a bunch of. I mean, I can see why men would get turned off.

HEATHER. But, we're making fun of ourselves. Didn't you get that? We're making fun of . . .

HEATHER, ALICE and CHERYL. of our types . . .

MANAGER. No. I didn't get that.

HEATHER. Well, maybe you'll get that in the song. (*To the* BAND.) Let's just do the song for him. You'll see, Joe, you'll see.

ALICE.
I'M DOING MY STRONG WOMAN NUMBER
WALKING WITH MY HEAD HELD HIGH
DOING MY STRONG WOMAN NUMBER
DETERMINATION IN MY EYE
I'VE GOT THE LOOK OF ASSURANCE
MY OBSERVATIONS HAVE PITH

AND THE ONE THAT I LOVE THINKS I'M
 WONDERFUL
BUT I'M NOT THE ONE THAT HE'S WITH

(CHERYL *is up on a stool behind* HEATHER *and* ALICE *doing
a subtle finger snapping samba routine.*)

 ALICE and HEATHER.
SO I'M DOING MY STRONG WOMAN NUMBER
I'M KEEPING IN THE BLOOM OF HEALTH

DOING MY STRONG WOMAN NUMBER
FIXING EVERYTHING MYSELF

I KNOW HOW TO MAKE A DECISION
MY OPINIONS ARE MY OWN
AND THE ONE THAT I LOVE THINKS IT'S
 WONDERFUL
THAT I CAN GET ALONG ALONE

 ALICE.
'CAUSE HE KNOWS I'LL NEVER BE A BURDEN
I WON'T HANG ON HIS SLEEVE
I'M SO SELF-SUFFICIENT
I'M SO EASY TO LEAVE
 (*Music continues under as she speaks.*) Do you know
what Frank said to me the last time he was in town?— He
said, "I wish my wife were more like you so I could leave
her." (*They scream in outrage.*) Let's face it. No man is
going to say, "Look at her, she's terrific—she builds her own

bookcases. Or— I love you because you fix your own faucets."

HEATHER. True. So true. I was going with a guy who claimed to be an equalitarian—well, he was, intellectually anyway—and one day he said to me wistfully, "You know, I really miss stockings and garter belts . . . They were such a turn-on." Well, you can't wear stockings and garter belts while you are building your own loftbed.

ALICE. You see, there's something we don't know here.

HEATHER. Something is fucked.

ALICE. I think it's us.
I CAN FIX MY OWN FAUCETS

HEATHER.
I CAN PLAN MY OWN LIFE

ALICE and HEATHER.
MAYBE WE'RE LOOKING IN THE WRONG
    DIRECTION
MAYBE WE NEED A WIFE!
(JOE *leaps up in dismay.*)
I'M DOING MY STRONG WOMAN NUMBER
AND OH, I'VE GOT SUCH SELF-ESTEEM

HEATHER.
I CAN HANDLE ANY CRISIS

ALICE.
I'M SO CAPABLE I COULD SCREAM

ALICE and HEATHER.
I'VE GOTTEN MY WHOLE LIFE TOGETHER
RECONSTRUCTED IT BIT BY BIT
BUT AS FOR FINDING LOVE, MY FRIEND,
THIS STRONG WOMAN NUMBER . . .
DOESN'T MEAN A SHIT!!

HEATHER. You see, there's just so much we don't know. Probably Jim's wife is just trying to establish her own identity—that's why she doesn't empty the cat box. It's probably a political statement. She is no doubt someone I would truly like if I really got to know her.

ALICE. No doubt.

HEATHER. She's probably just trying to get herself together—and to do that she has to totally rebel from Jim who has always controlled her life.

MANAGER. (*Bursting onto the scene.*) *It's hostility, that's what it is!* The reason she doesn't empty the cat box is ballbreaking hostility! I've been there, baby, and I know. (HEATHER *and* ALICE *and* CHERYL *are taken aback by the* MANAGER's *intrusion.*)

HEATHER. Uh, Joe, this is still part of the act.

MANAGER. I don't care if it's part of the act! Women are getting very hostile these days. Do you know why there are so many faggots out on the streets? It's because women are getting so hostile. A man can't trust a woman any more. The only place he's safe is with another man. I mean it's not my cup of tea, but I can certainly understand it.

HEATHER. Uh, Joe, do you want us to go on or what?

MANAGER. I just have to get a few things straight. My whole life is falling apart. Just understand that.

HEATHER. Right . . . so do you want me to go ahead?

MANAGER. What's the use? We're going to have to throw out all this stuff anyway and go back to the old act.

HEATHER. I don't want to go back to the old act! That's the whole point! I'm tired of my old act!

MANAGER. But I signed you on the basis of the old act and now you're giving me something completely different. I don't know what to do with this. See, that's what women do. You think you know what you're getting and then they change the ground rules on you. You never know where you stand. Francesca used to worship me. Jesus, I could do no wrong. She made me feel like a king. She taught me to open up and love. And it was beautiful. God, it was beautiful. And now it's shit. It's shit and I don't know what happened. I search and I search to find out what went wrong. I did my best. I tried to give her everything she needed. She wanted to be a painter so I encouraged her. I gave her money for lessons. I didn't want her to work, I just wanted her to be able to paint and develop herself. I told her I'd give her a studio. So she started painting and she was pretty good. Then she started hanging around with other painters down at the Art Students League. She started getting sloppy around the house—leaving her paint rags all over everything. Never fixing a meal. I didn't mind so much about the meals. Hell, I like Chinese food. And I got a cleaning lady, so she could just devote herself to her painting. I mean you can't expect an artist to be neat I figured. Then she got into some mystical shit and then one day she tells me she has a lover. She said it was someone she'd known in a former life and that it's something she needed to work out in this life. So I tried to be understanding and told her to go ahead and work it out, thinking it was a phase, thinking that I wanted her to grow and develop herself, and thinking that I didn't want to be labeled a male chauvinist pig. I gave her the studio so she could concentrate on her work, and then, this morning, when I got back, I went to the studio and there she was on the floor doing it with someone else and it wasn't even the one she'd known in a former life! This was another one—some guy she had modeling for her. And it was my money paying for his fee! I started realizing that I was the sucker of the year. Sucker! Sucker! There are a lot of us suckers out there trying not to be chauvinists and what happens? We get dumped on. Dumped on. The only answer is to be a faggot. (HEATHER *goes to him, patting his knee.*)

HEATHER. Well . . . if that's what will make you happy . . .

MANAGER. I didn't say it would make me happy! Do you think I *want to* be a faggot? . . . It's just that it's hard to find a good woman. Impossible actually. Actually it's probably impossible to have a good relationship of any kind. If I became a faggot I'd just mess it up.

HEATHER. I know, I know. (*She puts her arm around him to comfort him.*)

MANAGER. So maybe I should just be a recluse. A hermit.

HEATHER. I know how you feel. I've come to that too. (*She still has her arm around him.*)

MANAGER. I feel like I never knew Francesca.

HEATHER. I know, I know. See that's what women do. They don't let their men know who they are.

MANAGER. If I'd known who she was I wouldn't have married her.

HEATHER. That's why we don't let the men know who we are. They wouldn't want us if they knew. My husband never knew me. My ex-husband, I mean. If he'd known who I was he wouldn't have wanted me.

MANAGER. How do you know that?

HEATHER. Well, *you* don't want me the way I am.

MANAGER. Well, if you're doing stuff like that Strong Woman shit and that other offensive shit, I guess you're right.

HEATHER. See, that's exactly what I mean. So I tried to be a fantasy person, the perfect wife. I wanted to make him happy and so I tried to be who he wanted.

MANAGER. Well, that's not so bad. At least you were trying.

HEATHER. But it wasn't honest . . . I was the Good Girl right up to the end. I was so good. The last supper right before he left I fixed a well-balanced meal—roast beef, green beans and mashed potatoes. He felt guilty as hell leaving Mrs. Perfect. Poor thing. But I drove him to it because I didn't want him any more and hadn't for some time, but I was too much of a coward to leave myself. I had to manipulate things so that he would finally do the leaving while at the same time still appearing to be the good wife. I didn't even let myself know what I was doing. It was utterly devious and disgusting behavior. And he was the one left with the load of guilt. I should have written him a letter of apology. But I didn't. I wrote him a song instead. (SCOTT *begins the piano intro as if on cue and* HEATHER *smiles at him for picking it up. Speaking over intro.*) He was a good man . . .

DEAR TOM
YES, I ALWAYS FIXED YOUR SUPPER
DEAR TOM
YES, I GAVE MORE THAN I GOT
DEAR TOM
YOU THOUGHT THAT I WAS PERFECT
WELL, I'M NOT

DEAR TOM
YOU THOUGHT I WAS SO LOVING
DEAR TOM
YOU THOUGHT I WAS A SAINT
DEAR TOM
YOU THOUGHT THAT I WAS PERFECT
WELL, I AIN'T

ALL THOSE YEARS YOU WERE LIVING WITH
    SOMEONE
WHO WAS HIDING BEHIND A SMILE
ALL THOSE YEARS I WAS SOMEONE ELSE
DECEPTION WAS MY STYLE

I CLOSED YOU OUT BY ASKING FOR NOTHING
CAUSE I NEEDED SOMEONE TO BLAME
YOU COULDN'T GIVE WHAT I DIDN'T ASK FOR
IT WAS A PERFECT GAME

DEAR TOM
PERHAPS WE COULD HAVE MADE IT
DEAR TOM
BUT SOMEHOW WE WERE CAUGHT
DEAR TOM
IF WE WERE STARTING OVER
BUT WE'RE NOT

(JAKE, *as* LAWYER, *delivers the following on microphone.*
   HEATHER *picks up a divorce decree and is reading it as*
   JAKE *speaks.*)

LAWYER. Agreement made this 15th day of December,
1972, by and between Heather Applegate Jones—hereinafter
called the wife—and Thomas Murray Jones—hereinafter
called the husband. In consequence of unhappy differences,
the wife and the husband have heretofore separated and are
now living separate and apart, and since their separation
have agreed to live separate and apart for the rest of their
lives. This is in consideration of the fact that the (HEATHER
joins JAKE *reading.*)

LAWYER and HEATHER. husband never really wanted to
be married in the first place but was coerced into the marriage bond by the social pressures of the times, the expecta-
tions (JAKE *fades out.*)

HEATHER. of the day, and the inquiries by friends and relatives as to "When are you two going to get married?" After the marriage the husband began to wonder at the sudden end of his youth and resented having to do the little household tasks which his mother had always performed for him. The wife felt the resentments, was terrified that the husband would leave, felt compelled to try to make him happy, and therefore picked up his socks for him and never confronted him with her unhappiness at his unhappiness and adopted a cheery manner to convince herself and the husband that everything was all right. She even developed a kind of baby-talk—the personality of a lunatic-child—to use when she criticized his habits, so as not to risk his anger. (*Speaking in a kind of baby-talk, like Lily Tomlin's little girl impression—the speech of a charming mental retard.*) Thomas, this morning I came into the bathroom and I noticed that some person had left all their socks on the floor and cuds of hair in the sink and a ring around it from where they have shaved and I'm trying to figure out who did it. And I just wondered if you could help me figure out who did it . . . 'Cause if we find out we have to tell that person to pick up their socks and clean out the sink because the other person who lives there goes into the bathroom and gets her feet all caught up in the dirty socks and just might fall down and hit her head on the dirty sink and die. And you wouldn't want that to happen to her, would you? (*End baby talk.*) And the wife found that she was spending more and more time speaking as the child lunatic in order to pacify and manipulate her husband, until at times she felt she was becoming the child lunatic. At times it seemed that was the only way she could relate to her husband. The years passed with this charade until the two were strangers.

DEAR TOM

I WISH THAT I HAD KNOWN YOU

DEAR TOM
I WISH THAT YOU'D KNOWN ME
DEAR TOM
I HOPE THAT WE LEARNED SOMETHING
WELL, WE'LL SEE . . .

MANAGER. That's a nice song.

HEATHER. Thank you.

MANAGER. It's not a ball-breaker.

HEATHER. Thank you.

MANAGER. Maybe we can use it if we just cut the rap in the middle—especially the baby-talk part. It gets too personal.

HEATHER. But didn't you get the point of that?! About how we so totally cover ourselves, how we pretend to be another person in order to have a relationship—

MANAGER. I got it, I got it. But babe, it's bizarre. I mean, why do you want to tell people about that?

HEATHER. Why not?

MANAGER. Listen. We gotta talk. We gotta talk about what we're doing here. Listen, guys, take five then we'll get through the rest of this.

HEATHER. Hey, Jake, get me something from the deli.

JAKE. Anything?

HEATHER. Yeah. (*The* GROUP *disperses quietly.*)

MANAGER. (*To* HEATHER, *indicating a stool he has put Center Stage.*) Sit. Look, babe, we got to do something about all this.

HEATHER. About what?

MANAGER. What do you mean about what? It's your opening night, babe, and we got problems.

HEATHER. Oh, I thought you meant we have to do something about *all* of this—I mean, you were telling me about Francesca and we were talking about life—I'm sorry about your . . . problems.

MANAGER. Listen—those are the breaks, you know what I mean? We'll deal with life in a little while—after we've figured out what you're going to do in your act.

HEATHER. But I'm the one who has to figure that out, aren't I? It's *my* act.

MANAGER. Yeah, but I'm your manager and I'm the one who knows if your act is gonna work or not. If it's gonna sell out there across the country.

HEATHER. But isn't there a question of integrity here?

MANAGER. Sweetheart, what good's it gonna do if you've got integrity and nobody buys it. With this kind of integrity you may find yourself performing at home in your living room for a group of 23 close friends. Seventeen will buy the album. Is that what you want? I thought you were out there trying to *communicate* with people, trying to reach a lot of people.

HEATHER. That's what I'm trying to do.

MANAGER. Well, this isn't the way to do it. You've got to give 'em what they want first and then when you get acceptance you can sort of sneak up on 'em with your honest shit. And then they'll buy it.

HEATHER. But I'm tired of having to sneak up on people with my honest shit! For years I did that and it was disgusting. As a person I did it, and then I started playing Mary Stevens on the tube, and she was just like that. But now I'm not that person any more, and I want it all out front.

MANAGER. But the stuff you're putting out there is too personal. Nobody wants to hear that.

HEATHER. *You're* the one! You're the one who doesn't want to hear it! Because it threatens you. I know you, Joe. You are afraid to deal with a real, live woman. Look at Francesca.

MANAGER. That's not true! I crave a real, live woman. I've been through such crap. I just don't want a ball-breaker.

HEATHER. See! See! You want *your* idea of what a woman should be, not a real woman.

MANAGER. Are you saying that a real woman is a ball-breaker?

HEATHER. What do you think? Do you think that's what

I'm saying? No, that's not what I'm saying. You're not listening to me. Here I am, putting myself out there, the way I am, and you don't want it. You don't accept me the way I am. I mean personally. You don't accept me as a person . . . And it's my birthday.

MANAGER. Oh, Jesus. I knew that was still bothering you. Thirty-nine is a heavy trip. (*He tries to comfort her and she pulls away.*)

HEATHER. It is not a heavy trip! I'm not upset because I'm thirty-nine. I'm upset because it's my birthday and a person should be accepted on their birthday. It's a celebration that they were born—*that they are who they are!* And you don't want who I am! Face it! (HEATHER *is going berserk and* JOE *realizes he's got to try to get her to pull herself together.*)

MANAGER. Jesus . . . Yes I do. I think you're a wonderful person.

HEATHER. You do not.

MANAGER. I do.

HEATHER. You do?

MANAGER. I do.

HEATHER. What is it about me that you think is wonderful?

MANAGER. Well, I really like your voice. It's dynamic. And I like your delivery—very, uh, honest. And some of the stuff you write is very . . . telling. That's good. I'd say that's a plus. And I like your looks. Your looks are very . . . interesting. I mean, that's what I think personally. I always have.

HEATHER. What about the lines in my face.

MANAGER. They're very good. I like them.

HEATHER. You're lying.

MANAGER. No, it's the truth. Maybe it's a little weird on my part, but I like them. I can handle your lines. They add . . . uh . . . texture. And besides, with the lights—

HEATHER. You see! . . .

MANAGER. Okay, okay, we don't have to fix them with the lights. We'll just leave them the way they are.

HEATHER. Thank you . . . And what about my mind?

MANAGER. I like it. I like it very much. It's, uh, full of surprises.

HEATHER. And what about my strength. Is that a turn-off?

MANAGER. No, no, no, no, no. It's terrific. Your strength is very . . . uh . . . strong.

HEATHER. And my power. I have power, you know. Power—from the French *pouvoir*, meaning *to be able* to do something. To be able to effect change. Not power in the sense of power over people. Oh, no. Power, meaning to be able to do something. I have that.

MANAGER. Yes, well I like that. I like your strength and power.

HEATHER. You do?

MANAGER. I think it's great for a woman like you to have strength and power—independence. The ability to take care of yourself. I could use a little of that from a woman. Francesca, for instance. Francesca is a child. She is so dependent on me. I don't know what she'd do without me. I guess she'd die. She said that. After I threatened to leave her after I found her on the floor this morning with uh, you know—

HEATHER. The one she knew from a former life.

MANAGER. No, no, the model . . . The kumquat she was painting, sort of—well, she begged me not to leave, she fell on the floor hysterically and tried to pull out her own hair and said she would kill herself if I left. So I couldn't leave. You're not like that.

HEATHER. No . . .

MANAGER. You're strong. You can handle things.

HEATHER. Right . . . Look, Joe, I know I'm strong, but sometimes I just despair. I guess that's what you're seeing right now—despair. Isn't that interesting—that from time to time I've let you see me in despair. I don't let many people see that.

MANAGER. Well, thank you. That means a lot. Despair is okay. I enjoy it.

HEATHER. You're my friend, Joe. We have our differences, but we're still friends. I mean, I can come to you when I need to be in touch with a . . . sort of . . . sympathetic macho viewpoint.

MANAGER. Yeah, I know. I've got this tough macho exterior, but underneath I'm a cream puff.

HEATHER. I wrote a song about you. I'm doing it tonight. (*She starts playing the piano.*)

MANAGER. Jesus . . . Is it offensive?

HEATHER. (*Plays.*) No, it's very sympathetic. It's for the cream puff.
EVERY TIME I'VE LOST ANOTHER LOVER
I CALL UP MY OLD FRIEND
AND I SAY, "LET'S GET TOGETHER,
I'M UNDER THE WEATHER—
ANOTHER LOVE HAS COME TO AN END."
AND HE LISTENS AS I TELL HIM MY SAD STORY
AND WONDERS AT MY TASTE IN MEN
AND WE PONDER WHY I DO IT
AND THE PAIN OF GETTING THROUGH IT
AND HE LAUGHS AND SAYS, "YOU'LL DO IT
 AGAIN."

AND WE SIT IN A BAR AND TALK 'TIL TWO
ABOUT LIFE AND LOVE AS OLD FRIENDS DO
AND TELL EACH OTHER WHAT WE'VE BEEN
 THROUGH—
HOW LOVE IS RARE AND LIFE IS STRANGE

AND NOTHING LASTS AND PEOPLE CHANGE
AND I ASK HIM IF HIS LIFE IS EVER LONELY
AND IF HE EVER FEELS DESPAIR
AND HE SAYS HE'S LEARNED TO LOVE IT
'CAUSE THAT'S REALLY ALL PART OF IT
AND IT HELPS HIM FEEL THE GOOD TIMES
    WHEN THEY'RE THERE

AND WE SIT IN A BAR AND TALK 'TIL TWO
ABOUT LIFE AND LOVE AS OLD FRIENDS DO
AND TELL EACH OTHER WHAT WE'VE BEEN
    THROUGH—
HOW LOVE IS RARE AND LIFE IS STRANGE
NOTHING LASTS AND PEOPLE CHANGE

AND WE WONDER IF I'LL LIVE WITH ANY
    LOVERS
OR SPEND MY LIFE ALONE
AND THE BARTENDER IS DOZING
AND IT'S GETTING TIME FOR CLOSING
AND WE FIGURE THAT I'LL GO IT ON MY OWN.

BUT WE'LL MEET, THE YEAR WE'RE SIXTY-TWO
AND TRAVEL THE WORLD AS OLD FRIENDS DO
AND TELL EACH OTHER WHAT WE'VE BEEN
    THROUGH—
HOW LOVE IS RARE AND LIFE IS STRANGE
AND NOTHING LASTS AND PEOPLE CHANGE
HOW LOVE IS RARE AND LIFE IS STRANGE
AND NOTHING LASTS AND PEOPLE CHANGE . . .

MANAGER. That's beautiful . . . You're a wonderful woman.

HEATHER. Thank you.

MANAGER. You know, when I look at it objectively, I'd say you are one of the most wonderful women I've ever known. You're strong, even when you're in despair, you have perspective— You know, to tell the truth, I wish . . .

HEATHER. What . . . ?

MANAGER. I wish my wife were like you . . . so that I could leave her. (HEATHER *utters a cry of outrage and takes a punch at him.*) Oh Jesus, I meant that as a compliment.

HEATHER. Everything is so screwed up! You think I'm so wonderful, right?!—

MANAGER. Right. That's what I said.

HEATHER. But the qualities that make you think I'm so wonderful are the ones that would make you want to leave me.

MANAGER. I didn't say that—

HEATHER. They're the qualities that would make you want to leave me if you were even with me in the first place—

MANAGER. I didn't say that—

HEATHER. Which you aren't, of course, because you wouldn't even want a person like me because you can't really handle a woman with strength and power.

MANAGER. I told you I love your strength and power.

HEATHER. You may love it from afar, but you don't want it with you!

MANAGER. I was talking about my wife—

HEATHER. You'd rather be with someone who falls on the floor and pulls her hair out. You wouldn't want a person like me.

MANAGER. I didn't say that.

HEATHER. Well, would you? Could you ever in your wildest dreams conceive of being with a person like me?

MANAGER. Look, babe, I'm your manager. I'm your friend, but we have to keep it in bounds. We have to keep a little distance here. That was our agreement after . . . It's not that I wouldn't like to . . .

HEATHER. That's a cop-out.

(SOME *of the* GROUP *return from their break carrying a birthday cake with 40 candles on it.* ALICE *is carrying the cake followed by* JAKE *and* CHERYL.)

BAND.
HAPPY BIRTHDAY TO YOU
HAPPY BIRTHDAY TO YOU
HAPPY BIRTHDAY DEAR HEATHER
WE SURE DO LOVE YOU

(HEATHER *is still angry at* JOE, *but is trying to respond to the cake.*)

HEATHER. Oh, that's really nice, you guys.

ALICE. We love you.

CHERYL. We bought out the entire candle supply in the deli. Forty candles.

JAKE. Shut up, turkey. Make a wish, Heather.

MANAGER. Forty? She's only thirty-nine.

JAKE. One to grow on.

MANAGER. Well, let's not push it. Thirty-nine is fine.

HEATHER. It is not fine! You don't think it's fine. If you think thirty-nine is so bad what do you think is going to happen when I hit forty? My ass will fall off? (JAKE *does a sound effect with his guitar.*)

MANAGER. Sweetheart, nothing like that. You're in terrific shape. I'm just talking about your image.

HEATHER. So what's going to happen to my image?

JAKE. Heather, shut up and blow out the candles. I love you. Will somebody blow out these candles? All right, I am going to blow out these candles. (JAKE *blows out all the candles.*) And now for my next number . . . You know what I wished, Heather? That you'd turn around and look at me and take me seriously and realize that we could have a beautiful time together. I mean, here I am, young and vital and charismatic—you're not going to find any old dudes your age who understand where you're coming from. You might as well forget it. I mean, look at me—what more do you need? I'm unorthodox, uninhibited, supportive, and accessible.

MANAGER. Well, there's an offer you can't refuse.

JAKE. (*Sings an impromtu song and accompanies himself on his guitar. The lights dim and a spot comes in on him.*)
IN A SIMPLE WAY I LOVE YOU
I'M HERE TO SEE YOU THROUGH
I'LL MAKE MUSIC WHILE YOU SING YOUR SONG
WHILE YOU DO WHAT YOU HAVE TO DO
I'LL BE BESIDE YOU
RAIN OR SHINE
LOVE HAS MANY FACES
AND ONE OF THEM IS MINE

MANAGER. (*Yelling out to the* LIGHTING PERSON.) Lights, lights! That wasn't a number. He was just fooling around. I know it's confusing. (*The lights come back up and the* REST OF THE BAND *comes in.*)

HEATHER. Thanks, Jake.

JAKE. That's what I get. Thanks, Jake. Look, is it because I'm so much younger than you? Does that hang you up?

HEATHER. It does not hang me up!

JAKE. I mean, I think forty is a very exciting age in a woman.

HEATHER. Thirty-nine. Let's not rush it.

MANAGER. Look, let's get on with this. What's the next number, sweetheart?

HEATHER. Well, you're not going to like it, but I don't care.

MANAGER. Honey, you're so insecure. So defensive.

HEATHER. I'm not defensive! I'm an angry person!

MANAGER. All right, all right. You're an angry person. Just do your number.

HEATHER. (*Yells up at the* LIGHTING PERSON.) Isabella! This is a number! (*This number is a trio—flashy.* HEATHER, *the* TWO BACK-UP SINGERS, *and* BAND.)

TRIO.
SOMEBODY'S FIXING ME UP
SOMEBODY'S DRAWING A FACE ON ME
SOMEBODY'S WANTING TO WRITE MY ACT
THE WAY THEY THINK IT OUGHT TO BE
SOMEBODY'S DRESSING ME UP
AND MAKING ME LOOK MIGHTY GOOD, SO I'M
    TOLD
AND EVERYBODY SAYS THIS IS HOW IT'S DONE
I'VE BEEN PUT IN A PACKAGE AND SOLD

ALICE.
SOMEBODY'S DOING MY HAIR

CHERYL.
SOMEBODY'S DRAWING A SMILE ON ME

HEATHER.
AND SOMETIMES I WONDER WHAT IT IS
THAT SOMEONE EVER SAW IN ME

TRIO.
SOMEBODY'S DRESSING ME UP
AND MAKING ME LOOK MIGHTY GOOD, SO I'M
    TOLD
AND EVERYBODY KNOWS IT'S PART OF THE
    GAME
TO BE PUT IN A PACKAGE AND SOLD

HEATHER.
AND IF YOU COME AND BUY ME
AND PICK ME OFF THE SHELF
YOU'LL GET THE STUFF THEY THINK YOU
    WANT
BUT IT WON'T BE MYSELF
'CAUSE

TRIO.
SOMEBODY'S CHANGING MY STYLE
SOMEBODY'S HANGING A LOOK ON ME
SOMEBODY'S WONDERING IF I'LL SELL
AND IF SOMEONE CAN MARKET ME
DOO, DOO, etc.

HEATHER.
AND IF NOBODY BUYS ME
AND LEAVES ME SITTING ON THE SHELF
I'LL STILL WRITE THE SONGS THAT PLEASE ME
AND SING 'EM TO MYSELF

TRIO.
'CAUSE NOBODY'S CHANGING THE WORDS
AND NOBODY'S CHANGING THE MELODY
AND NOBODY'S CHANGING WHAT'S IN MY HEAD

HEATHER.
OR THE FEELINGS I GOT INSIDE OF ME
SO LISTEN TO MY SONG
AND DUMP ALL THE REST BY THE SIDE OF THE
　　ROAD
AND LOOK INSIDE FOR THE PART OF ME
THAT CAN'T BE PUT IN A PACKAGE AND SOLD
CAN'T BE PUT IN A PACKAGE AND SOLD
CAN'T BE PUT IN A PACKAGE AND SOLD
　　How does that grab you?

MANAGER. It's cute. It'll work.

HEATHER. It will?

MANAGER. It's sexy. I know you're probably trying to be obnoxious, but I kind of like it. You're cute when you're mad.

HEATHER. I don't believe I heard that. (*From someplace Off-Stage* SOMEONE *calls.*)

OFF-STAGE VOICE. Phone for Joe Epstein.

MANAGER. Heather, honey, calm down. I'm telling you I like that number. We can use it.

HEATHER. But you like it for the wrong reasons!

MANAGER. Look, I like it. It doesn't matter why.

HEATHER. Yes, it does!

OFF-STAGE VOICE. Is Joe Epstein out there? Phone.

PIANIST. Phone, Joe.

MANAGER. Tell 'em I'll call back later.

PIANIST. (*Yelling.*) He'll call back later.

OFF-STAGE VOICE. It's his wife.

PIANIST. It's your wife.

MANAGER. Oh, shit . . . Tell her I'll call back later. Look, Heather, about tonight—what we can do is use some of the old act and then use some of the new numbers—like this one, and the one about me, and the "Dear Tom" number without the rap in the middle—

OFF-STAGE VOICE. She says she just tried to commit suicide and needs for you to come home right away.

MANAGER. What?

PIANIST. She says she just tried to commit suicide and needs for you to come home right away. Is your wife a joker or something?

MANAGER. Jesus! . . . Where's the phone? (*He runs Off.* EVERYBODY *stands stunned, not quite knowing how to react.*)

PIANIST. I hope it's nothing serious. (*The* MUSICIANS *laugh uneasily.*)

JAKE. What should we do? Run something down?

HEATHER. Yeah, I guess we might as well work on one of our numbers while Francesca is doing her number. (*The* MUSICIANS *make a low murmur, as though pointing a "Bad Girl" finger at* HEATHER.) Okay, okay, I'm a terrible person. (HEATHER *does a* FRANCESCA *imitation.*) Joe this is your little wife Francesca. Oh, Joe, I'm in such despair. I just can't live without you. I think I'm just going to have to commit suicide by pulling all my hair out. When you come to the funeral I'll be bald. (*She falls down on the floor, pulls out her hair and "dies."*)

JAKE. You are a terrible person.

(JOE *comes back in.* ALL *are aware.* HEATHER *pulls herself up. We hear a slight "Oh" from* HEATHER.)

MANAGER. I've gotta get home pretty soon.

HEATHER. Joe, is she okay?

MANAGER. Yeah, she's just a little shaken up. Her wrists are bleeding. She, uh, couldn't find the vein. It's all my fault. This morning when I left I said I was leaving for good. Jesus, I never thought she'd do it.

HEATHER. Well, she didn't.

MANAGER. What do you mean she didn't?

HEATHER. Well, she didn't really kill herself.

MANAGER. Well, she sure as hell tried. She just couldn't find the vein.

DRUMMER. You know there are better ways to do it. I had a friend—

JAKE. Shut up, turkey.

DRUMMER. No, I'm serious. He put on some Jimi Hendrix, turned it up loud and hanged himself. When they found him in the morning the music was still playing. It was very dramatic.

BASS. Remember that woman in Florida who did it on television?

MANAGER. Hey, fellahs, please—I gotta go, and we've gotta decide some things before tonight—

JAKE. C'mon, everybody. The dude's in pain . . .

MANAGER. I never thought she'd do it. I don't understand women. I guess she needs me. The bottom line is she needs me. I've tried. I've given her everything and still she tries to kill herself. What does she want? What am I supposed to do? She acts depressed. I'm trying to make her happy, she doesn't want to do any little things that would make me happy, she finds another lover—

HEATHER. Two. One from a former life and—the kumquat.

MANAGER. Okay, two. And when I threaten to leave she tries to kill herself. So what am I supposed to do?

HEATHER. Well, maybe she's just going to have to kill herself.

MANAGER. I don't believe you said that—

HEATHER. If that's what she wants—

MANAGER. She doesn't want to!

HEATHER. So what does she want?

MANAGER. I don't know! She doesn't know. God if she did it, I could never forgive myself. I could never face myself in the mirror again. I'd be responsible.

HEATHER. No, you wouldn't! That's her number she's doing.

MANAGER. She's not doing a number.

HEATHER. So why aren't you leaving at top speed? The

reason you're not leaving at top speed is you know she's doing a number.

MANAGER. Okay, I'm leaving. She's not doing a number. She's just a little confused. She's actually a very delightful, intelligent, loving girl. You've never understood that, Heather. And she needs me.

HEATHER. I think you just have a very sick relationship.

MANAGER. Sick!? It's not sick! . . . I asked my analyst if it was sick and he did not say it was sick.

HEATHER. Well, you yourself said it was shit.

MANAGER. That's very different. It may be shit, but it's not sick. We have our problems . . .

HEATHER. You're just both doing a number! That's what's happening! You want it this way! Everything is so fucked up!

JAKE. Hey, Heather, calm down.

MANAGER. Why are you so angry at *me*? I don't understand women.

HEATHER. You see, men would rather have a shitty thing than a good thing. It's less binding. As long as a relationship is shitty, they have a sense of freedom because they can say to themselves, "This is shitty and I really should get out of it." But if a relationship is good, that's very frightening, because then they don't have an excuse to get out. So the trick becomes to stay in a relationship and keep it shitty so the door is always open. Face it, you would not want to lose your shitty relationship.

MANAGER. Heather, you used to be such a nice person—

HEATHER. Well, I'm not nice anymore! (*To* JOE.) Can't you see that she's just manipulating you?!

MANAGER. She's not manipulating me—she doesn't know what she's doing, and I've got to get her straightened out somehow. She's just a child.

HEATHER. She knows what she's doing! Women know how to manipulate instinctively. It has been the only way we could get power! I did it and it was disgusting. Now I'd rather yell and scream. At least that's honest.

MANAGER. It's not too attractive.

HEATHER. Well, is it attractive to slice your wrists up and bleed all over everything? Is that what's appealing to you? You see! You like that. You'd like to believe that she needs you so much she'd kill herself without you. You like that, don't you? It's appealing. This is appealing. (*She demonstrates cutting her wrists and bleeding all over everything.*)

MANAGER. I have to get home. My notes. (*He hands her his notes.*)

HEATHER. We are all in such a mess! We have so much garbage in our heads! You see, I just don't think it's possible. It's just not possible— (*The* MUSICIANS *join in—they've heard this before.*)

68

HEATHER and MUSICIANS. —to have a decent constructive relationship with anybody—

HEATHER. (*Yelling at them.*) Well, it's not!

(JAKE *starts playing heavy blues chords and sings with an old-time blues fervor. A spotlight comes up on him and down on* EVERYBODY ELSE *as though he is doing a number.*)

JAKE.
SOME PEOPLE JUST TOO SHORT
SOME PEOPLE JUST TOO TALL
SOME PEOPLE ONLY GOT MORE OR LESS
AND SO NOTHING CAN WORK OUT AT ALL

IF ONLY THINGS WAS DIFFERENT
LIFE WOULD WORK OUT FINE
IF ONLY THINGS WAS DIFFERENT
LIFE WOULD WORK OUT FINE

IF ONLY I WASN'T TWENTY-FOUR
AND YOU WASN'T
O-O-O-O-O-O-O-O-O-O-
THIRTY-NINE!

MANAGER. Lights! —That wasn't a number either. (*The lights bump back up.*)

HEATHER. (*Shading her eyes and looking out to the*

Lighting Person.) Isabella, I know you're having trouble telling what's a number and what isn't. I'm sorry. (*She whirls back to the* Band.) Look, Jake, I know you're making fun of me, but it's true. Does anybody here have a really good constructive love relationship? . . . Let's see a show of hands.

Drummer. I'm too short.

Pianist. I'm too skinny.

Bass. I have a good constructive relationship.

Manager. I've got to get home. My wife needs me.

Heather. So go! Leave!

Manager. This is what you're going to do tonight: go back to your old act—you can use the opener of this act if you want to—

Heather. I'm not going back to the old act.

Manager. Your old act was terrific. It was sweet. It was nice. It worked. The new act doesn't work. It's angry and confused and offensive.

Heather. That's because I'm angry and confused and offensive. That's who I am!

Manager. Well, who wants to see that?

Heather. I don't know!

JAKE. Look, people might dig it. I do. It's a trip. It's an odyssey, man. Besides, it's not offensive. It's touching. I like it. It's brave.

MANAGER. So how do we sell bravery? Look, Heather, I can't do it. Either you go back to the old act or I gotta split. I don't know what to do with you.

HEATHER. So go ahead and split.

MANAGER. But it's your opening night, babe. And it's important. All the big people in the industry are going to be here, all the DJ's, the guys from Billboard, Cashbox, Newsweek. They're gonna think you're crazy. They're gonna think *I'm* crazy.

HEATHER. Go ahead and leave. Keep your shitty relationship.

MANAGER. But, babe, we've worked together a long time. I hate to see it all go down the drain. You're destroying yourself.

HEATHER. Go home to your wife. I can get along.

MANAGER. You're making this seem personal.

HEATHER. It is personal! You don't want me—you want some other person.

MANAGER. I'm having trouble handling this whole thing. This day is possibly the worst day of my life. All the women in my life have gone berserk. My professional life is going down the drain and my personal life is going down the drain.

HEATHER. You see, I just don't know if it's worth it. I've been trying to cut through the crap of the past—I've been trying to drop all the disguises, and finally here I am standing naked before you and what do I get—rejection! That's because you're not ready for me. Admit it!

MANAGER. I admit it. (*She tries to punch him, pushing him down to the floor. She straddles him.*)

HEATHER. You see! You're not ready for the new woman. Right?

MANAGER. Right.

HEATHER. I have such a rage! (*She starts hitting him. He is a little stunned. He lies there while she is on top of him.*) How can you just lie there and admit that you're not ready for the new woman without feeling some remorse?

MANAGER. I feel remorse. Definite remorse.

HEATHER. And don't you feel a sense of loss?

MANAGER. . . . If this is a sample of what I'm missing I can't honestly say I feel a sense of loss.

HEATHER. How long do you think it's going to be before you're ready?

MANAGER. Ready for what?

HEATHER. The new woman!

MANAGER. I'd say about two decades.

HEATHER. You drive me crazy! You see, I thought it could work with us, Joe. I thought, "If I could just get through to him."— But I can't and I feel such despair! We can't make it. The whole thing is hopeless. (*She climbs off* JOE.) If you can't give me room to grow, you've gotta get out of my life.

MANAGER. You're doing this to yourself, babe. I simply can't manage you this way.

HEATHER. I know. I'm unmanageable.

MANAGER. So why are you doing this to yourself?

HEATHER. For my own self-esteem.

MANAGER. It's an ego trip. Well, looks like the new woman has made her bed and now she's going to have to lie in it!

HEATHER. Right!

MANAGER. Alone.

HEATHER. Look, man, I've been alone before. I've been alone since I was two years old. I was alone when I was married. That's what my act is all about—being alone. So go ahead and leave! I don't need you, Joe! I don't need you!

MANAGER. I hate to see this happening, babe. We've been through so much.

HEATHER. Leave!

MANAGER. Okay, okay. If that's the way you want it. I guess this is something you've got to do. I think it's a big mistake, but . . . well, good luck, babe. You're a talented person. (*He kisses her quickly on the shoulder and leaves.* HEATHER *stands there alone. She calls after* JOE.)

HEATHER. That's right, Joe! It's what I have to do! I can't do anything else! (*Pause.*) Let's just go on.

(*The lights continue to change. The* BAND *crashes in with a rhythmic driving beat.* EVERYONE *is singing but* HEATHER.)

ALICE, JAKE and CHERYL.
GOTTA FEEL THE LOVE
YOU GOTTA GET TO IT
GOTTA FEEL THE PAIN
IF YOU'RE GONNA GET THROUGH IT
    (HEATHER *joins:*)
YOU CAN'T RUN AWAY
YOU WON'T FIND A PLACE TO HIDE
LET IT BE, LET IT GO
LET IT BE, LET IT GO
LET IT RIDE—

HEATHER.
FEEL THE THING INSIDE
(*Alone. The lights come down to a spotlight on her. She sings with no musical accompaniment.*)
I HAVE BEEN A LONELY LADY ALL MY LIFE

AND TO TELL THE TRUTH I'M SCARED OF
    FINDING HOME
I REMEMBER MOMMA CRYING IN THE NIGHT
AND MAKING DESPERATE CALLS ON THE
    PHONE
I REMEMBER CREEPING DOWN THE HALL BY
    THE DOOR
I REMEMBER LISTENING ON THE STAIR
I REMEMBER WONDERING IF THEY LOVED
    EACH OTHER ANY MORE
I REMEMBER FEELING SUCH DESPAIR

I HAVE BEEN A LONELY LADY ALL MY LIFE
AND TO TELL THE TRUTH I'M SCARED OF
    FINDING HOME
IT SEEMS SO VERY HARD TO MAKE LOVE TURN
    OUT RIGHT
SOMETIMES I THINK I'M BETTER ON MY OWN
(*The accompaniment from the* BAND *creeps in, gradually*
    building.)
I'VE GOT THESE ARMS THAT CAN REACH OUT
I'VE GOT THESE EYES THAT CAN SEE
I'VE GOT THIS VOICE THAT CAN SING
CELEBRATION OF ME
AND I DON'T KNOW WHAT'S COMING
BUT THIS NEW DAY FEELS FINE
'CAUSE I WOKE UP THIS MORNING
AND THE FACE IN THE MIRROR WAS MINE

  ALICE and CHERYL.
HAPPY BIRTHDAY
HAPPY BIRTHDAY, HAPPY BIRTHDAY

HEATHER, ALICE and CHERYL.
HAPPY BIRTHDAY, HAPPY BIRTHDAY

HEATHER.
I'VE GOT THESE FRIENDS I CAN COUNT ON
AND THEY CAN LOVE AND LET BE
I'VE GOT THESE FEET THAT CAN DANCE
CELEBRATION OF ME
AND I DON'T KNOW WHAT'S COMING
BUT I AM MY OWN DESIGN
AND MY WHOLE LIFE IS A POEM
AND THE WORDS AND THE RHYTHMS ARE MINE

HEATHER, ALICE and CHERYL.
HAPPY BIRTHDAY, HAPPY BIRTHDAY
(*In echoes.*)
HAPPY BIRTHDAY, HAPPY BIRTHDAY

HEATHER.
THIS IS THE DAY I WAS BORN
THIS IS THE DAY I BEGIN
WITH THE RAIN STILL TAP-DANCING ON MY
    HEAD
THE SUN IS STARTING TO GRIN

HEATHER, ALICE and CHERYL.
HAPPY BIRTHDAY, HAPPY BIRTHDAY
HAPPY BIRTHDAY, HAPPY BIRTHDAY

HEATHER.
AND I DON'T KNOW WHAT'S COMING
BUT THIS NEW DAY FEELS FINE
'CAUSE I WOKE UP THIS MORNING
AND THE FACE IN THE MIRROR WAS MINE

HEATHER, ALICE and CHERYL.
//HAPPY BIRTHDAY, HAPPY BIRTHDAY
  HAPPY BIRTHDAY, HAPPY BIRTHDAY//
(*Repeat.*)

HEATHER.
ALL I NEED IS A LITTLE ROOM
A PLACE THAT IS FINE AND FREE
A ROOM WHERE I CAN THINK TO MYSELF
WHERE NOBODY'S NEEDING ME

AND THEN I'LL FIND MY WAY AGAIN
AND I WILL SING MY SONG
AND I'LL FIND THE JOY AGAIN
THAT COMES WHEN I'M FEELING STRONG

SO TOMORROW I HIT THE ROAD
GONNA LET LOOSE OF THIS HEAVY LOAD AND

ALL.
FLY

MUSIC IS MY ONE SALVATION
SINGING IS MY CELEBRATION
AND PLAYING WITH A ROCK 'N ROLL BAND IS A
    NATURAL HIGH.
OOOHHH OOH OOHH OH OOOH
OOOOHHH OOH OOHH OH OOOHH
OOOHHH OOH OOHH OH OOOHH
OOOHHH OOH OOHH OH OOOHH

(*The music begins to fade, as if a little rock 'n roll band is going off down the road.* HEATHER *signals to the* SPOTLIGHT OPERATOR *to dim the lights. The spot irises out on her.*)

THE END